ZAC POWER

hardie grant EGMONT

Close Shave
first published in 2014
this edition published in 2017 by
Hardie Grant Egmont
Ground Floor, Building 1, 658 Church Street
Richmond, Victoria 3121, Australia
www.hardiegrantegmont.com.au

A CiP record for this title is available from the National Library of Australia.

Illustrations by Craig Phillips
Illustrations inked by Latifah Cornelius
Design by Simon Swingler

Printed in China through Asia Pacific Offset

1 3 5 4 2

CLOSE SHAVE
BY H.I. LARRY

ILLUSTRATIONS BY CRAIG PHILLIPS

hardie grant EGMONT

CHAPTER

It was early on Saturday morning, and Zac Power was waiting outside his local HairCo store. Using all of his secret agent stealth, he slipped through the crowd and peered into the shop window.

For weeks, he had been waiting. Saving his pocket money. Counting down. And now the day was finally here!

HairCo were the makers of Super-Strength Hair Gel, Zac's favourite hair product. Even though Zac was really busy with his spy work for the Government Investigation Bureau (GIB for short), he always made sure his hair looked cool.

Today HairCo was releasing a brand-new hair gel called UltraHold. The ad on TV said the new gel had a chemical that made it twice as strong as the old one. This would really come in handy on Zac's long missions.

Zac checked his watch.

8.56 A.M.

In four minutes, the shop would open and UltraHold would go on sale.

There was a huge crowd of people behind Zac, all waiting to get their hands on a tube of the new hair gel.

Zac checked the reflection in the shop window to make sure no-one from school was standing behind him. It was an old spy trick he'd picked up at Spy School. He might have been proud of his hair, but he still didn't want his friends to catch him queuing up to buy hair products.

Then Zac's SpyPad beeped. A SpyPad was the gadget carried by every GIB agent.

It was a phone, a computer and a GPS tracker all in one. It also had all the latest games installed. Zac had a message from his mum.

Zac, don't forget you have a haircut tomorrow.
Love, Agent Bum Smack

Zac groaned. He hated having his hair cut. But before he could reply to his mum, the shop doors finally opened. The crowd flooded inside.

Zac grabbed a tube of UltraHold and rushed up to the counter to pay for it. It cost him a month's worth of pocket money.

Oh, well, thought Zac. *It'll be worth it when my hair looks good for a whole mission!*

As he unscrewed the lid, Zac heard a guy shouting from the other end of the shop. But the crowd was so big and loud that he couldn't make out what the guy was saying.

Zac squeezed some of the hair gel out of the tube. It was sticky and blue and cold in his hand.

What's so different about this new formula? he wondered. *It looks just like the old gel.*

He looked across the crowd again. That guy was still shouting, and it sounded like he was coming closer. Zac could hear some of what he was saying now.

'Stop! Don't use that hair gel! Throw it away!'

Yeah, right, thought Zac. *I've been saving up for this stuff for weeks! As if I'm going to throw it away.*

Then the shouting guy burst out of the crowd. It was Leon, Zac's older brother.

'Zac, no!' Leon shouted. 'Whatever you do, don't –'

But it was too late. Zac was already smoothing the gel through his hair.

'Oh, Zac,' Leon sighed. 'You're going to wish you hadn't done that.'

CHAPTER 2

'What are you talking about?' Zac asked, wiping his hands on his jeans. 'What's the big deal?'

'I can't tell you here,' said Leon, grabbing Zac by the arm. He dragged him through the crowd and out of the shop.

Zac rolled his eyes. Leon always took everything so seriously! Like Zac, Leon was a GIB spy. But Leon was in charge of gadgets and vehicles – he never went on missions.

Just as well, thought Zac. *All that stress would probably give him a heart attack!*

Leon led Zac out into the street and down an empty alley. They finally came to a stop next to a dirty old dumpster.

'OK,' said Zac impatiently, 'now can you tell me what's going on?'

Leon kept glancing at Zac's hair as though he thought it might explode. 'Here,' he said. 'Read this.'

He dropped a little silver disk into Zac's hand. A new mission!

Zac pulled out his SpyPad and slipped the mission disk inside.

CLASSIFIED
MISSION INITIATED 9 A.M.

The evil Dr Drastic has taken over the HairCo factory in Bladesville City. He is using the factory to produce a new hair gel known as UltraHold.
This gel contains a chemical that causes permanent hair loss. Anyone who uses it will go completely bald after 24 hours. The antidote is being held at the HairCo factory.

YOUR MISSION
- Travel to Bladesville City.
- Get to the HairCo factory and find Dr Drastic.
- Get the antidote to UltaHold gel.
~ END ~

Zac ran his hands through his hair. He was going to *go bald*?

'Calm down,' said Leon. 'The hair gel takes 24 hours to start working, and you will have completed the mission by then.'

'OK,' said Zac, trying not to worry.

He had run into Dr Drastic before. That crazy old doctor was always coming up with evil plans to make people miserable. But this was the worst thing Dr Drastic had ever done!

'I don't get it,' said Zac angrily. 'Why is Dr Drastic doing this? What's in it for him?'

'Money,' said Leon. 'He's making all this money selling UltraHold...'

'And then he's going to force people to buy his antidote and make even more money,' finished Zac.

'Right,' said Leon. 'Unless you can get into that factory and stop him.'

'OK,' said Zac. He wanted to get on with his mission straight away. 'What have you got for me?'

'I'm transferring the co-ordinates of the HairCo factory to your SpyPad now,' said Leon. 'Now, Bladesville is a big city, so you'll need a way to get around.'

Leon reached into his backpack and pulled out a heavy blue block.

Zac raised an eyebrow. 'I'm going to ride around on a brick?'

'It's not a brick,' said Leon. 'It's a Super-Compact Short-Range Hoverboard. It just folds down into this shape to make it easier to transport.'

'Oh,' said Zac. 'So how do I unfold it?'

'It's voice activated,' said Leon. 'Well, song activated, actually.'

'What?'

'When you get to Bladesville, all you have to do is sing a particular song and the hoverboard will unfold and zoom straight over to you,' said Leon. 'I've set it to respond to *Earthquake* by Axe Grinder. You like that song, right?'

Zac groaned. 'Why would you make it song activated?' Then he glared at his brother, suddenly suspicious. 'You just thought it would be funny to make me sing in public, didn't you?'

'Er, no.' Leon grinned, not quite meeting Zac's eye. 'Song activation is much more secure than simple voice activation. It's much harder to match the pitch, tone and tempo of a *musical* encryption.'

'Whatever, Leon,' said Zac, rolling his eyes. He shoved the hoverboard into his backpack and glanced down at his watch.

9.19 A.M.

'Anything else?' he asked Leon.

'One more thing,' said Leon, pulling some kind of jumpsuit out of his bag. It was bright pink.

'No way,' said Zac firmly. 'I don't care what it does, I'm *not* putting that on!'

'Don't worry,' said Leon. 'It doesn't look like this all the time.'

He held up one of the sleeves. There was a keypad on it. 'This,' he said proudly, 'is the latest in disguise technology – the Shift Suit!'

Leon pushed a button. The pink jumpsuit shimmered for a second. And suddenly, it wasn't pink anymore. It was blue. A blue police uniform.

'There are over 500 clothing options,' said Leon, pushing another button. The Shift Suit shimmered again, and this time it turned into a gleaming white lab coat.

'Awesome,' said Zac, impressed. 'How does it work?'

'It's quite simple, really,' said Leon. 'The fabric is made up of thousands of strands of tiny nanobots which can re-pattern themselves according to commands from the —'

'Never mind,' said Zac, sorry he'd asked. Leon could go on for hours! 'So how am I getting to Bladesville? On that brick hoverboard thing?'

Leon shook his head. 'The hoverboard only has a limited battery life, so you'll want to leave it switched off until you reach the city. I've got another vehicle for the first leg of your trip.'

'Oh,' said Zac. 'Where is it?'

Leon pointed to the filthy dumpster they were standing beside. 'You're looking at it.'

CHAPTER

Zac looked at the dumpster. 'No, really. Where's my ride?'

'Just trust me and get in,' Leon said with a grin. He reached up and flipped open the dumpster's lid.

'I'm not jumping into a bin!' said Zac.

'Well, you could always *walk* to Bladesville,' suggested Leon.

Zac sighed. *The things I do for GIB*. He grabbed the edge of the dumpster and hoisted himself up over the side.

WOOMPH!

Zac landed on something soft and squishy. But it wasn't rubbish. He was sitting in a comfortable leather chair.

Zac looked around and saw that he was behind the wheel of a sleek sports car.

The image of a dumpster was projected around it as a disguise. The dumpster flickered, and a second later the disguise was gone.

Through the window, Zac saw Leon laughing at him.

'This is the Holo-Racer 5000,' Leon

explained. 'The next generation in covert vehicle technology.'

'You know, you could have *told* me the dumpster was a hologram before you shoved me into it,' said Zac.

'Where's the fun in that?' Leon grinned.

Zac rolled his eyes. Secretly, he thought the Holo-Racer was cool, but he wasn't going to tell Leon that.

'The Holo-Racer is completely voice activated,' Leon added. 'Just tell it where you want to go, then sit back and enjoy the ride!'

'Well, at least it's not *song* activated,' Zac said under his breath, strapping his seatbelt on. Then he leant into the microphone on the dashboard and said, 'Uh, Bladesville City?'

SCREEEEECH!

The car tore down the alley, away from Leon. Zac didn't even have time to wave goodbye — the Holo-Racer had already zoomed around the corner.

Zac rocketed through town and out onto the highway, weaving between the other cars at breakneck speed.

For a while, he couldn't see anything but open road. But then he spotted buildings rising up in the distance. It was Bladesville City.

As the Holo-Racer drove along, Zac checked the map of Bladesville on his

SpyPad. It seemed he should be able to drive right up to the HairCo factory.

But as Zac got closer to the city, he realised it wasn't going to be that simple. Up ahead, a long line of cars was blocking the road. The Holo-Racer rolled smoothly to a stop behind them.

Zac could just make out a set of broken traffic lights blinking on and off way off in the distance. A single policeman was standing in the middle of the road, directing the traffic with his hands. It was taking forever!

Zac glanced at his watch.

11.42 A.M.

At this rate, he was never going to get

to the factory in time.

Zac leant over to the Holo-Racer's microphone and said, 'Pull over.'

The car immediately pulled off to the side of the road, coming to a stop behind some trees.

As soon as Zac got out, the hologram flickered back into place around the Holo-Racer. But this time, instead of a dumpster, the car was disguised as a big leafy bush.

Clever, thought Zac. He reached into his backpack and pulled out the hoverboard.

'I can't believe it's song activated,' he muttered to himself. Then, checking to make sure that no-one was around, Zac took a deep breath and began to sing. '*When I play my guitar it's like an earthquake!*'

The brick dropped out of his hands and landed on the grass.

CLICK-CLICK-CLICK!

A metal rod shot up from the top of the brick and two handles unfolded out of the end. At the same time, a pair of foot-sized platforms slid out from the sides.

Zac kept singing.

'*Coz I rock so hard I make the whole world shake!*'

WHIRRRRRR!

The hoverboard rose into the air and hovered towards Zac. He grinned to himself and stepped on the platforms.

Leaning forward on the handles, he shot out from behind the trees and back to the highway.

Bladesville City, here I come!

CHAPTER 4

Unfortunately, Bladesville City turned out to be a lot further away than it had looked from the highway. And as fast as the hoverboard was, Leon had built it to navigate a city – not to travel long distances. Zac wasn't sure how long its battery would last.

By the time he reached Bladesville, the sun was beginning to set.

5.46 P.M.

Zac had been there before on other spy missions, but he'd forgotten how loud and crazy it was. Billboards flashed. Music blared. People bustled past, shouting into mobile phones.

Zac brought up the map of Bladesville on his SpyPad and began winding his way through the crowded streets. The city was like a maze, and before long, Zac had to stop in an alley to look closer at the map.

'Well, well,' said a cold voice from behind Zac. 'What have we here?'

Zac wheeled around. Three teenagers

were striding towards him. One was tall and skinny. The other two were big and ape-like. They all had hooded jumpers and boxer shorts sticking out of their jeans.

They grinned as they closed in on Zac. They were obviously looking for trouble.

Zac shook his head. These guys had no idea who they were dealing with. He quickly stepped off the hoverboard and stood in front of it.

'Nice video game,' said the skinny kid, eyeing Zac's SpyPad. 'I might take that.'

He snatched the SpyPad out of Zac's hands. The two big guys laughed.

'Aww, this isn't a game!' the skinny kid muttered, staring at the screen. 'It's just a stupid map!' He tossed Zac's SpyPad into the gutter.

Zac clenched his teeth. He was a karate master. He could have taken on all three of them with his eyes closed. But GIB agents were only allowed to use their fighting skills against enemy agents.

He slid his hand into in his backpack, hoping that there was something in there he could use to get rid of them. His fingers closed around a lightweight plastic tube.

Wedgie-Copter, thought Zac. *Perfect.* He'd forgotten that was even in there. He'd bought it at the GIB hardware store ages ago and had been planning to use it on Leon.

'What's that?' the skinny guy demanded as Zac pulled the gadget out of his bag. 'Give it to me!'

'Here,' said Zac with a smile. 'Let me show you how it works.'

He yanked the ripcord and the Wedgie-Copter buzzed to life, its propeller whirring. Zac let go and it flew through the air towards the boys.

'What are you doing?' the skinny kid yelped. 'What is that?'

But the Wedgie-Copter had already locked onto its target. It clamped down on the back of the bigger kid's undies and pulled them up so high that he was lifted into the air.

RRRIIIPPP!!

Then the Wedgie-Copter released the boy and he dropped to the ground.

'Run!' the boy shouted, getting to his feet and rubbing his bum.

The Wedgie-Copter snapped and whizzed as the boys ran down the street. Zac laughed as he watched them go. But as he reached down to retrieve his SpyPad from the gutter, he saw something that made him go cold.

The SpyPad's screen was dead.

Zac hammered the ON button, but nothing happened. It was broken.

If Leon were here, he could probably fix it in about two seconds. But Zac wasn't that good at repairing broken gadgets.

He was stranded in the middle of a big city with a broken SpyPad and only 16 hours left to stop Dr Drastic.

And without the map to show him the way, how would he ever find the factory?

CHAPTER 5

Zac steered the hoverboard into the main street, looking around desperately for some sign of the HairCo factory.

If only I knew someone who lived in the city, he thought. *Then I could ask them for help.*

Then Zac remembered that GIB had a contact in Bladesville named Mrs X. She was a crazy old lady who owned a place called the Electric Eel Workshop. She had helped Zac on another mission in Bladesville. Mrs X lived on the south side of the city, in a street called Dank Alley. Zac pulled the hoverboard around and rode off.

BEEP-BEEP! BEEP-BEEP!

Zac looked down at the hoverboard's control panel. *Now what?* he thought.

...WARNING: LOW BATTERY...

Uh-oh.

The hoverboard shuddered. Zac sighed and folded it back up into his backpack. He didn't want to use all the battery.

I guess this means I'm walking, he groaned to himself.

Zac raced through the city, hoping he was heading the right way. He thought he remembered the way to Mrs X's place, but the whole city was a blur of bright lights and loud music and for a while it seemed like he was just going in circles.

Then, finally, he came to a street that looked familiar. It was dark and grimy and smelt like rubbish. Steam rose up from the gutter, clouding the whole street. Zac glanced up at a glowing street sign.

DANK ALLEY

This was it! He checked the time.

9.02 P.M.

Zac raced up to the end of the alley and found the dirty grey door of Mrs X's shop.

'Mrs X!' he called, knocking on the door. 'It's Agent Rock Star. I need your help!' Rock Star was Zac's GIB code name.

Mrs X didn't answer. Zac wondered if she was even home. But then he heard the clanking of rusty deadlocks. The door was pushed open by a wrinkled arm with a giant eel tattoo.

'What you want?' Mrs X snapped. She had white hair and yellow teeth, and she spoke in an accent that Zac couldn't place.

'I'm looking for the HairCo hair gel factory,' said Zac urgently.

'HairCo factory?' Mrs X chuckled. 'You're long way from there, Mr Rock Star. But I think I got something to help.'

'Great!' said Zac. 'Er, can I come in?'

'No,' said Mrs X sharply. 'You wait.'

She slammed the door in Zac's face. Zac waited, staring back down the filthy alley. He ran a hand through his hair, just to make sure it was still there.

A few minutes later, the door flew open again and Mrs X held up a pair of sunglasses. 'Here,' she said.

'Cool shades,' said Zac, raising an eyebrow. 'But how are they going to help me find the HairCo factory?'

'These GPS,' said Mrs X, thrusting the sunglasses at Zac. 'Global Positioning Sunglasses. Take you anywhere you want.'

Zac slipped them on. 'Whoa!'

A line of blinking yellow arrows had appeared on the road in front of him, projected across his field of vision by the sunglasses. The arrows traced a path down the alley and around the corner.

From a speaker at Zac's ear, a computerised voice said, 'At the end of the road, turn left.'

'Very nice, huh?' said Mrs X. 'This latest technology. Very expensive. GIB owe me *big* money for this one!'

'Uh, OK,' said Zac, hoping GIB wouldn't be too upset by the enormous bill that Mrs X was sure to send them.

The old lady broke into an insane cackle and slammed the door shut again.

Zac didn't have any time to waste. The Global Positioning Sunglasses guided him in a zig-zagging path through the streets of Bladesville. He sprinted through crowded shopping centres, under a giant bridge, and down a long, wide street lined with factories.

As Zac got closer to the HairCo factory, the arrows changed from yellow to orange to red.

I must be getting warmer, he smiled to

himself. He kept moving until the line of arrows came to a stop outside a steel-walled building with glowing windows.

'You have reached your destination,' said the voice in his ear.

Finally, thought Zac. He took off the sunglasses and slipped them into his pocket.

Then something caught his eye and he realised that getting inside the HairCo factory wasn't going to be as easy as he'd hoped.

Standing outside the front entrance were two enormous guards.

CHAPTER

Zac crouched behind a parked car. He reached into his backpack and found Leon's Shift Suit.

Pulling the pink jumpsuit on over his clothes, he began searching for a disguise that might help him get inside the factory.

The little screen on the sleeve scrolled through a bunch of options:

Jet Pilot
Astronaut
Rock Star

I wish, thought Zac. Then he came across a costume that might be a bit more helpful.

Safety Inspector

That gave Zac an idea. He tapped the OK button and felt a weird tingling as the Shift Suit shimmered all around him. The pink nanobots changed colour, transforming into a fancy business suit.

Nice, Zac smiled, smoothing out his jacket. He started to stand up, but then he felt something moving at his collar. A second later, a bright red tie flickered into place around his neck.

Time to go, thought Zac, getting up.

He froze. The Shift Suit was tingling again. Zac's pocket gave a shake and a little ID badge flipped out onto the front of his jacket.

JOHN SMITH
Safety Inspector

'OK,' Zac muttered, staring down at his clothes, '*now* are you finished?' He stood up from behind the car and walked across the street to the HairCo factory.

The two guards stood blocking the front doors, arms folded in front of them.

They stared down at Zac as he came up the steps towards them.

'Hello, gentlemen,' said Zac, putting on a deep voice. 'I'm from the Bladesville Safety Council.'

'What do you want?' grumbled the guard on the left.

'I'm here to perform a surprise safety check on this factory,' said Zac.

'In the middle of the night?' said the guard on the right, looking very suspicious.

Zac's eyes flashed to his watch.

11.07 P.M.

'Er, yeah,' said Zac. 'Surprise!'

There was a long silence. The two guards looked Zac up and down.

'Why are you wearing those shoes?' grunted the guard on the left, pointing at Zac's feet.

Zac looked down. *Uh-oh.* He was still wearing his bright red sneakers. Not exactly normal safety inspector shoes.

'These are part of the uniform,' said Zac, thinking quickly. 'They're special safety shoes.'

'Sure they are,' smirked the guard on the right. 'Look, mate, if you think you can just walk in here and – hey, what are you doing?'

Zac had pulled out his broken SpyPad and was holding it up to his ear like a mobile phone.

'I asked you a question, mate,' the guard grunted. 'What are you doing?'

'Just making a phone call,' Zac lied.

The guard on the left glared at Zac. 'Oh yeah?' he said. 'And who are you calling?'

Zac held up a hand to silence him. 'Hello?' he said, speaking into the SpyPad. 'Is that Dr Drastic? Excellent. This is Safety Inspector John Smith.'

Zac paused, pretending Dr Drastic was talking on the other end. 'Yes, Dr Drastic, I'm here for a surprise inspection,' he said. 'Well, I'm *trying* to get in. But there are two guards out the front who won't let me through the door.'

Zac paused again. The guards looked sideways at each other.

'You're going to *fire* them if they don't let me in?' said Zac.

The guards' faces went white. 'No, wait!' said the guard on the left, reaching for the front door. 'Please don't –!'

'We're letting you in!' the guard on the right said quickly, waving Zac inside. 'See? Tell Dr Drastic we're letting you in!'

'Oh,' said Zac, still pretending he was on the phone. 'Hang on. It looks like they *are* letting me inside after all.'

'Yes, sir!' said the guard on the left. 'Of course we are!'

'We're so sorry to hold you up!' said

the guard on the right, smiling nervously.
'I hope you, uh, have a nice inspection!'

'Thank you,' said Zac, stepping between
them. 'Just don't let it happen again.'

'No sir!' said the two guards together.

Trying hard not to laugh, Zac left the
guards behind and walked in through the
front door of the HairCo factory.

CHAPTER 7

The factory doors closed behind Zac and he found himself in a small, dark room. In the distance, he could hear something big and mechanical working away.

SQUIRT-CLUNK-WHIRRR!

Following the sound, Zac slipped through a door into a long, wide corridor.

SQUIRT-CLUNK-WHIRRR!

At the far end, he found another door. The noise of the machine was getting louder. It had to be coming from behind the door.

SQUIRT-CLUNK-WHIRRR!

Zac opened the door a crack and peered through. There was nobody around. Then, opening the door wider, he gasped.

The room was as big as his school gym. And filling up almost the whole space was a huge machine. The whirring of gears and clunking metal was deafening.

A giant steel tank towered above Zac's head. Clear plastic pipes wormed out from the tank, carrying streams of Ultra Hold gel across the room.

The pipes ended in metal nozzles that squirted the gel into tubes. When the tubes were full, robotic claws swooped down from the ceiling to screw on the lids. Then the tubes were dropped into boxes and carried out of the room on a conveyor belt.

Zac checked the time.

11.30 P.M.

Zac snapped a quick photo as evidence with his watch. Then he stared at the machine, looking for a way to shut it down.

Tubes of hair gel shot past on a conveyer belt in front of him. He reached out a hand and grabbed one of them.

Suddenly, one of the robotic claws shot

down towards him from the ceiling. It snatched the tube out of Zac's hand, put it back on the machine, and screwed on a lid.

Zac grabbed another tube. This time, he moved right away from the machine until his back was up against the wall. But the claw followed him and pulled the tube out of his hand again.

They must have some kind of gel tube sensor, Zac realised. He stared up at the claw as it rose back towards the ceiling. *Probably to catch anything that falls off the machine.*

That gave him an idea.

Moving as fast as he could, Zac pulled five more tubes of hair gel off the conveyer belt. He stuffed them all into his pockets and ran as fast as he could towards the tank of hair gel.

Five more claws dropped down from the roof. Zac raced across the factory floor and the claws followed behind him at top speed.

That's right, thought Zac. *Come and get me!*

He reached the huge hair gel tank. There was a rusty ladder leading up to the top of the tank. Zac grabbed the sides and started climbing as fast as he could.

The robotic claws chased him all the way. One of them lunged at Zac's pocket, but Zac threw out his foot and kicked it aside.

You can have the tubes in a minute, he thought.

Zac reached the top of the ladder and crawled onto the lid of the tank. He found a little square hatch on the tank's roof.

Zac grabbed the handle and yanked the hatch open. There was bubbling blue goo inside. The hair gel! Zac could hear the robotic claws snapping behind him, so he quickly pulled the hair gel tubes out of his pocket and dropped them into the tank.

Just as he'd hoped, the claws kept on chasing the tubes. They dived through the hatch, splashing down into the blue goo. The whole tank shook as the claws clanked around inside.

Time to get out of here, thought Zac. He dropped back onto the ladder and slid down to the floor.

The hair gel machine was shuddering to a stop, all jammed up by the snapping claws. It gave a horrible grinding screech.

An alarm started blaring. Smoke hissed into the air. And then –

KABOOM!

The tank puffed out like a giant balloon and exploded, sending hair gel splashing down like rain all over the room. Zac dived out of the way just in time, taking cover behind a stack of cardboard boxes. He didn't want to get any more hair-loss gel in his hair!

When the shower of hair gel finally stopped, Zac stood up and looked at what was left of the machine. It definitely wouldn't be making any more hair gel.

A sudden noise behind Zac sent a chill up his spine. There was someone behind him – and they were *laughing*.

SPLOOSH!

Zac didn't even have time to turn around before something icy and wet smacked into the back of his head. His eyes fluttered closed and he fell to the ground.

CHAPTER

Zac drifted in and out of sleep. He was surrounded by cold water, making him feel very woozy.

When he finally woke up, Zac found himself lying on a concrete floor. His clothes were soaked through. The shift suit had changed back to a pink jumpsuit and the screen on the sleeve was dead.

Zac wriggled out of it quickly, rubbing his eyes, then slowly got to his feet and tried to figure out what was going on. He realised he was trapped in a glass cage in some kind of laboratory.

There were two enormous glass tanks across the room. One was filled with blue UltraHold hair gel, and the other with a different green gel. Between the two tanks was a massive funnel, almost as high as the roof. Sitting on top of the funnel, pointing straight up the ceiling, was a giant fan.

Zac glanced sleepily down at his watch.

8.41 A.M.

It's morning already, he thought anxiously.

He must have been asleep for hours!

Suddenly, Zac's hands shot up to his head. He breathed a sigh of relief as he realised that his hair was still there. But he had less than 20 minutes to finish his mission before his hair started falling out!

Zac heard footsteps and looked up. A man was walking out from behind the funnel thing, dragging a thick hose. He was wearing a lab coat and had crazy white hair that shot out in all directions.

Dr Drastic.

In his case, going bald would be an improvement, thought Zac.

'Oh,' said Dr Drastic, turning around. 'You're awake. Good.'

He stretched out the hose and plugged it into the side of the blue gel tank. Then he walked back over to the funnel and chuckled to himself as he tapped at a little keypad.

'What's so funny?' said Zac, folding his arms. 'I heard you laughing right before you knocked me out, too.'

Dr Drastic gave him a cold smile. 'It was funny,' he said. 'The look on your face. You actually thought you'd beat me.'

'What do you mean?' said Zac. 'I did a pretty good job of destroying your machine, didn't I?'

'Ha!' Drastic barked. 'That was just my packaging machine! I don't even care about that.' He swept an arm around his laboratory. 'This is where the *real* magic happens.'

Zac stared at Dr Drastic. Did that mean he'd made even more UltraHold hair gel? Zac looked around for his backpack, but it was gone. Dr Drastic must have taken it.

'What's that other gel for?' Zac asked, pointing at the green tank, playing for time. He had to think of a way to get out of there.

Dr Drastic didn't answer. He just walked back across to the blue tank and adjusted the giant hose.

Then Zac realised what the green gel was. 'It's the antidote, isn't it?' he asked.

'Never mind that now,' said Dr Drastic, giving Zac an irritated look. 'I have to get on with the next phase of my plan.' He pulled a remote control out of his pocket and pushed a button.

CREEEAAK!

With a loud creak, the ceiling above their heads slid open. Outside, Zac could see blue sky and towering buildings.

'You see,' said Drastic, '*selling* my hair gel was a good start. But not everyone uses hair gel. So I've come up with a much better way of spreading my evil UltraHold gel around.'

'Oh, yeah?' said Zac. 'And what's that?'

Dr Drastic pointed to the weird

machine with the funnel coming out of it. 'This is my new Vaporiser,' he said. 'It can turn this UltraHold hair gel into a thick fog. Then the fan pumps it out into the air.'

Drastic pulled a lever at the side of the Vaporiser and the gadget began to hum and whir.

'In a few minutes, the Vaporiser will pump out enough fog to cover this whole city. A few hours later, it will reach your home town. Within a week, it will spread through the entire country!'

Zac gritted his teeth and pressed his hands against the glass in front of him. He had to do something!

'Think of it!' Drastic shouted. 'Millions of people, all losing their precious hair. Then I can sell them my antidote and make billions of dollars!'

Dr Drastic's face grew suddenly cold. 'And you, Agent Rock Star, will never be given the antidote. You will be bald forever.'

CHAPTER 9

WHOOMPH! WHOOMPH!

Still trapped in the glass cage, Zac watched helplessly as the Vaporiser finished powering up.

Clouds of blue fog billowed up through the giant funnel. The fan spun to life, blowing the vaporised UltraHold gel through the open roof and out into the city.

Zac's eyes shot to his watch.

8.52 A.M.

Only eight minutes until he'd lose his hair forever! Zac had to escape from the glass cage and get hold of the antidote. If Dr Drastic was telling the truth, the fate of the entire country's hair was in his hands.

Then suddenly, Zac had an idea. But would it work? *Only one way to find out,* thought Zac, clearing his throat. He opened his mouth and began to sing. '*When I play my guitar it's like an earthquake!*'

Dr Drastic stared at him. 'Singing, Rock Star?' He shook his head. 'And they call me crazy.'

Zac ignored him and kept singing. '*Coz I rock so hard I make the world shake!*'

'Rock Star, what are you doing?'

WHIRRRRRR!

Yes! Zac thought triumphantly.

'What's that?' Drastic snapped.

The noise got louder and louder.

Suddenly, Zac's backpack came flying into the room. It rocketed towards him, bulging and wriggling, like there was something inside that was trying to get out.

RRRRIIIPPP!

Then Zac's hoverboard tore free of the backpack and expanded to full size. There was just enough battery!

CLICK-CLICK-CLICK!

The hoverboard zoomed towards the cage. Zac backed away from the glass and shielded his face.

SMASH!

The hoverboard shot straight through the glass wall in front of Zac, blasting a giant hole in it!

Zac climbed on the hoverboard and flew out of the smashed hole. He sped out into the laboratory.

BEEP-BEEP! BEEP-BEEP!

The hoverboard moved jerkily, its battery almost gone.

Dr Drastic's hand flashed to his back pocket. He pulled out some kind of high-tech shooter.

It was bulbous and blue, with a pointy yellow nozzle at the front. He pointed it at Zac.

SPLOOSH!

A blast of freezing cold water came shooting out of the weapon.

Zac ducked just in time. The blast whizzed past and hit the wall behind him.

With a loud crackling sound, the water froze up and turned to solid ice.

I guess that explains the puddle I woke up in, thought Zac. *Drastic must have hit me with that thing back in the machine room.*

'Do you like my Ice-olater, Rock Star?' taunted Dr Drastic. 'I invented it just to use on you.'

Zac ignored him and zipped across the laboratory towards a narrow ramp that went up around the Vaporiser.

SPLOOSH!

Zac ducked down as another blast of water came shooting past. He guided the hoverboard up the ramp.

SPLOOSH! SPLOOSH!

Two more misses.

Dr Drastic let out an angry shout and started running up the ramp after Zac.

The blue cloud of UltraHold fog drifted right across the ramp in front of Zac, blocking his path. He couldn't see anything beyond it. But he couldn't go back. Dr Drastic was chasing him.

Zac had no choice. He pointed the Hoverboard forward. It rattled, then jolted straight ahead, into the fog.

I'm already about to lose my hair, he thought firmly. *What's a bit more going to do to me?*

For a second, everything was a blur of blue. Then Zac burst out the other side of the cloud. But the ramp turned into a dead end! The only way out was to jump into the tank of bubbling blue UltraHold gel underneath, but there was no way Zac was doing that.

Zac groaned. All he could do was turn the hoverboard around and wait to see what Dr Drastic would do next.

SPLOOSH! SPLOOSH!

Dr Drastic fired madly through the fog from the other side, but he couldn't see what he was shooting at. None of the shots came anywhere near Zac.

Then the firing stopped. For a second, Zac thought that Dr Drastic had given up.

But then Zac heard footsteps along the ramp. Drastic came running out of the fog, his Ice-olator pointed straight at Zac. He cackled madly and pulled the trigger.

CHAPTER 10

SPLOOSH!

Without even thinking, Zac jumped down from his hoverboard and kicked it toward Dr Drastic.

The blast from the Ice-olator crashed into the hoverboard, turning it into a giant ice cube.

But the hoverboard ice cube kept

shooting through the air. It zoomed along the ramp and smacked into Dr Drastic!

Drastic staggered. He spun his arms, trying to get his balance back, but it was no good. He tumbled over the side of the ramp, splashing into the giant tank of UltraHold hair gel.

Zac peered down over the side of the ramp. He could see ripples on the surface where Dr Drastic had fallen in. A second later, Drastic's head popped up out of the pool.

He pulled himself up onto the side of the tank, slimy and gasping and...completely bald.

'No!' cried Dr Drastic, grabbing at his

shiny head. 'My hair! My beautiful hair!'

I thought that stuff was supposed to take 24 hours to kick in, Zac thought. *Guess it works faster if you go SWIMMING in it!*

Dr Drastic climbed out of the tank, dropped down to the ground and ran out of the room, sobbing. Zac couldn't help but feel a little bit sorry for him. It looked like Dr Drastic was serious about his own hair, too.

But Zac didn't have time to waste. He ran back down the ramp and raced across to the Vaporiser. He grabbed the lever that Dr Drastic had used to turn it on and heaved it in the opposite direction.

Nothing happened.

Why is it never that simple? Zac thought. He scanned the laboratory, searching for a Plan B. *Aha!*

He ran over to the blue tank and grabbed the massive hose that was sucking Ultra Hold gel into the Vaporiser. He pulled at the hose with all his strength.

POP!

The hose came free. Blue slime started gushing out of the tap on the side of the tank, splashing across Zac's feet.

Struggling not to slip over, Zac dragged the hose across to the green tank and plugged it in.

WHOOMPH! WHOOMPH!

The Vaporiser shuddered. It started to

suck up the green gel. A minute later, the fog began to change colour, turning a deep shade of green. The Vaporiser was now pumping the antidote out into the city.

Zac's eyes darted down to his watch.

8.59 A.M.

He might have saved the city, but he still hadn't saved his own hair!

Only one minute left!

Zac sprinted back across the lab. He bolted up the ramp to the green tank and leant over the side to dunk his whole head into the antidote gel. Then he stood up, wiped the gel off his forehead, and breathed a long sigh.

He'd never been so relieved to complete

a mission! He wasn't going to go bald after all.

On his way back down the ramp, Zac caught a glimpse of his reflection in the side of the green tank. He stopped walking and spent a couple of minutes spiking up his hair.

Perfect, he thought, grinning at himself in the glass. *Drastic may be an evil madman, but this gel has excellent hold!*

A few minutes later, Zac walked out through the front doors of the HairCo factory. The two security guards were still keeping watch outside.

'Well, did you finish your inspection?' asked one of them as Zac came past. 'Is the factory safe?'

Zac grinned at them. 'It is now.'

He walked down the stairs and then stopped as he heard footsteps thundering towards him. He turned and saw his brother coming up the street, followed by two other GIB agents.

'Leon?' Zac raised an eyebrow. 'What are you doing here?'

'Back-up,' said Leon. 'Just in case.'

'Why would you think I needed back-up?' said Zac.

'Your SpyPad *did* drop out of contact for 16 hours,' Leon pointed out. 'Besides, we all know how you get when someone messes with your hair.'

Zac pulled out his broken SpyPad and handed it to Leon. 'I'm fine,' he said, as Leon started poking at it with a screwdriver. 'But that thing's completely busted. I finished the mission and —'

'Here you go,' Leon smiled, handing back the SpyPad. 'It's fixed.'

Zac rolled his eyes. Leon was a big nerd, but he did come in handy sometimes.

The second that Zac switched on his SpyPad again, it began to ring.

Zac hit the answer button. His mum's face filled the SpyPad screen.

'There you are!' said his mum. 'Thank

goodness you're — *what happened to your hair?'*

'It's just gel, mum,' said Zac, rolling his eyes.

'You did that *on purpose?'* his mum asked, raising her eyebrows. 'It looks ridiculous. Thank goodness you're getting a haircut.'

Zac sighed as he hung up the SpyPad. He'd forgotten his mum had booked him in for a haircut today. She always did that, just when he was starting to like the way his hair looked.

Oh well, Zac thought, catching a glimpse of his cool hairstyle in a window. *At least I still have hair for the hairdresser to cut!*